White Fang

Jack London

Condensed and Adapted by
CLAY STAFFORD

Cover and Illustrations by
JERRY DILLINGHAM

Dalmatian Pr

The Junior Classics have been
adapted and illustrated with care and thought
to introduce you to a world of famous authors, characters, ideas,
and great stories that have been loved for generations.

Editor — Kathryn Knight
Creative Director — Gina Rhodes Haynes
And the entire classics project team
of Dalmatian Press

WHITE FANG

Copyright © 2013 Dalmatian Press, LLC,
an imprint of Dalmatian Publishing Group.
Franklin, Tennessee 37067 • 1-866-418-2572
dalmatianpress.com

Printed in the United States of America

A note to the reader—

A classic story rests in your hands. The characters are famous. The tale is timeless.

This Junior Classic edition of *White Fang* has been carefully condensed and adapted from the original version (which you really *must* read when you're ready for every detail). We kept the well-known phrases for you. We kept Jack London's style. And we kept the important imagery and heart of the tale.

Literature is terrific fun! It encourages you to think. It helps you dream. It is full of heroes and villains, suspense and humor, adventure and wonder, and new ideas. It introduces you to writers who reach out across time to say: "Do you want to hear a story I wrote?"

Curl up and enjoy.

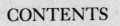

CONTENTS

CHARACTERS

BILL AND HENRY — two dogsledders

FATTY, FROG, SPANKER, ONE EAR —
dogs on Bill and Henry's team

SHE-WOLF — White Fang's mother, who is
half dog, called Kiche by the Indians

ONE EYE — a wolf, White Fang's father, who
is blind in one eye

WHITE FANG — (The Fighting Wolf, Wolf)
the gray cub, who survives the trials of the Wild
and life at the hands of man-animals

MOTHER LYNX — gives the she-wolf and the
gray cub a tough fight

GRAY BEAVER, KLOO-KOOCH, MIT-SAH —
the Indian man and his family, who own Kiche
and White Fang

LIP-LIP — a bully among the Indian dogs and
White Fang's rival

BASEEK — the first full-grown dog White Fang faces down

BEAUTY SMITH — White Fang's second owner, a cruel coward who enjoys seeing dogs fight

TIM KEENAN — the owner of the bulldog, Cherokee, that fights White Fang

WEEDON SCOTT — the master who truly cares for White Fang

MATT — a dog-musher who helps Weedon teach White Fang

JUDGE SCOTT — Weedon's father, who cannot quite trust a wolf

MRS. SCOTT, BETH AND MARY — Weedon's mother and sisters

ALICE — Weedon's wife

WEEDON AND MAUD — Weedon's children

White Fang

CHAPTER ONE

The She-Wolf

Down the frozen waterway pawed a string of wolfish dogs. Ice clung to their fur, and their breath froze in the air. Leather harnesses were on the dogs, and leather traces attached them to a sled which dragged along behind. On the sled, securely tied, was a long and narrow box.

One man worked ahead of the dogs, on wide snowshoes. Another man worked at the back of the sled. Their bodies were covered with fur and soft leather. Their eyelashes and cheeks and lips were coated with ice from their frozen breath. On the sled, in the box, lay a third man whose work was over—a dead man.

They traveled without talking. On every side was silence. An hour went by, and a second hour. The pale light of the sunless day was beginning to fade. A faint, far cry arose on the still air. Then another. The front man turned his head until his eyes met the eyes of the man behind.

"They're after us, Bill," said the front man.

"Meat is scarce," answered his friend. "I ain't seen rabbit tracks for days."

After this, they spoke no more.

When it got dark they made camp. The wolf-dogs gathered on the far side of the fire.

"Henry," asked Bill, munching on beans, "how many dogs have we got?"

"Six."

"Well, Henry… We've got six dogs. I took six fish out of the bag. I gave one fish to each dog an', Henry, I was one fish short. I had to go back to the bag to get One Ear a fish."

"We've only got six dogs," Henry said.

"I won't say they was all dogs," Bill went on, "but there was seven of 'em that got fish. I saw the other one run off across the snow."

"I'll be almighty glad when this trip's over."

"What d'ye mean by that?" Bill demanded.

"I mean that you're beginnin' to see things."

"The tracks is there in the snow," Bill answered. "I'll show 'em to you."

"Then you're thinkin' it was—" A long wailing cry from somewhere in the darkness interrupted him. "—one of *them*?"

Bill nodded.

From every side the cries arose and grew louder. The dogs huddled closer to the fire.

"Henry, I was a-thinking…" said Bill. "That man there in the box is a sight luckier than we'll ever be. Long distance funerals is something you an' me can't afford. Why a man as rich as him wanted to come up here is more than I can see."

Bill started to speak, but then pointed out toward the wall of darkness. There they saw a pair of eyes gleaming like red coals. Then a second pair. Then a third. The sled dogs became afraid and rushed over to the men.

"Henry, it's real unlucky that we're out of rifle cartridges."

Henry stopped spreading blankets. "How many cartridges did you say you had left?"

"Three. And I wish it was three hundred!" Bill shook his fist at the gleaming eyes.

The men crawled into bed and slept, side by side, under one covering. The fire died down, and the gleaming eyes drew closer. The dogs huddled in fear. Once the dogs' cries became so loud that Bill woke up. He got out of bed and threw more wood on the fire. As it began to flame up, the circle of eyes drew farther back. He glanced at the huddled dogs and rubbed his eyes.

"Henry," he said.

Henry groaned, "What's wrong now?"

"There's seven of 'em again."

Not really hearing, Henry grunted and drifted back to sleep.

In the darkness of the morning, Henry made breakfast, while Bill made the sled ready.

"Say, Henry," Bill called, "one of the dogs is gone! Now there's only five."

Henry rushed over and counted the dogs. "You're right. Fatty's gone. Just like that? They couldn't jes' swallow him alive..."

"We didn't hear nothin'," Bill added.

"Surely he didn't run off. Not out there. Not to them. What would make a dog follow after them? That would be killing his fool self."

"But Fatty's gone, sure as the world."

The men launched into the darkness. They heard the wolves howling all day long.

That night, Henry was adding ice to cool the bubbling pot of beans. He was suddenly startled by a shout from Bill and a snarling cry of pain from among the dogs. Looking, he saw Bill amid the dogs. In one hand he held a stout club, in the other the chewed tail of a sun-cured salmon.

"It got half of it," he announced, "but I got a whack in just the same."

"What'd it look like?" Henry asked.

"Like any dog."

"Must be a tame wolf."

——— • ———

The next morning, Bill shouted, "Frog's gone."

Henry counted the dogs, and then joined his partner in cursing the wolves that had robbed them of another dog.

"Frog was the strongest of the bunch," Bill said.

They ate a gloomy breakfast. Then they harnessed the four remaining dogs to the sled. The day was the same as the others before—all work and silence, except for the wailing wolves.

That night, Bill not only tied up the dogs, but he also tied them so they couldn't chew themselves free.

"If we could put a couple of shot into 'em," Henry remarked, "those wolves would be more respectful."

A sound among the dogs attracted the men's attention. Full into the firelight glided a doglike animal. It moved slowly, watching the men, then fixing its eyes on the dogs.

"That fool One Ear don't seem scairt much," Bill said in a low tone.

"It's a she-wolf," Henry whispered back. "She's the decoy for the pack. She draws out the dog. Then the other wolves pitches in an' eats him up."

The fire crackled. A log fell apart with a loud spluttering noise. At the sound, the strange animal leaped back into the darkness.

"Henry, I'm a-thinkin'," Bill said, "that was the one I whopped with the club."

"It knows for certain more than a self-respectin' wolf ought to know," Henry agreed. "A wolf that knows enough to come in with the dogs at feedin' time has been around people."

"Part dog, for sure," said Bill.

In the morning, Henry renewed the fire and cooked breakfast.

As soon as Bill sat down to eat, Henry said, "Spanker's gone."

Bill counted the dogs. "How'd it happen?"

Henry shrugged his shoulders. "Don't know. One Ear must have chewed Spanker loose."

"I'll tie 'em up out of reach of each other tonight," Bill said.

They took to the trail, anxious to reach the town of McGurry—and to be rid of the hungry wolves that followed just out of sight.

As the cold gray of the afternoon came on, Bill slipped the rifle from under the sled lashings.

"You keep right on, Henry," he said. "I'm goin' to see what I can see."

"You'd better stick by the sled," his partner replied. "You've only got three cartridges."

Bill didn't listen. He disappeared into the gray quiet. An hour later, he came back to the sled.

"The wolves are scattered wide, lookin' for other game and followin' us. They're thin. They ain't had nothin' to eat in weeks, I reckon, except our dogs. There's so many wolves, *that* didn't feed 'em much."

A few minutes later, Henry, who was now behind the sled, gave a low, warning whistle. Bill turned and stopped the dogs.

"It's the she-wolf," Bill whispered.

Just behind them on the trail trotted a furry, slinking wolf. The animal came forward a few steps. It repeated this several times, till it was a short hundred yards away.

"Biggest wolf I ever seen," Henry commented.

"Kind of a strange red color," Bill answered, "like a husky. Hey, hey, come here, you husky!"

"Ain't a bit scairt of you," Henry laughed.

Bill waved his hand and shouted, but the animal showed no fear. The men were meat and the wolf was hungry.

"We've got three cartridges," Bill said. "It's a dead shot. She's killed three already. The dogs will want to follow her 'cause she's part dog. What do you say I shoot it?"

Henry nodded. But before Bill could get the rifle to his shoulder, the she-wolf leaped into a clump of spruce trees and disappeared.

"I might have knowed it," Bill said. "A wolf that knows enough to come in with the dogs at feedin' time would know all about guns."

They camped early that night. Before they went to bed, Bill saw to it that the dogs were tied out of gnawing-reach of one another.

But the wolves were growing bolder.

"They're goin' to get us," Bill remarked as he listened to the growls and the fire-crackle.

"They've half got you already, a-talkin' like that," Henry retorted sharply. "A man's half-licked when he says he is. And you're half-eaten from the way you're goin' on."

CHAPTER TWO

The Hunger Cry

The day began well enough. They had lost no dogs during the night. They swung upon the trail and darkness with lighter spirits. Bill even made a few jokes when the sled accidentally overturned.

With the sled upside down, they had to unharness the dogs to straighten out the tangle. Henry saw One Ear creeping away.

"Here, you, One Ear!" he cried.

But One Ear broke into a run. And there, out in the snow, was the she-wolf waiting for him. She moved toward him a few steps, playfully, and then halted. Every step forward that he took, she took one back.

Too late, One Ear learned his mistake. A dozen wolves bounded across the snow. The she-wolf snarled and sprang. One Ear thrust her off and tried to circle back toward the sled.

"Where are you goin'?" Henry demanded, laying his arm on Bill's arm.

"I won't stand it," Bill said. "They ain't a-goin' to get any more of our dogs." Gun in hand, he plunged into the underbrush.

"Don't take no chances!" Henry called after him. He sat down on the sled and watched.

All too quickly, Henry heard three shots and he knew that Bill's ammunition was gone. One Ear yelped. A wolf cried out. And that was all. Silence.

Henry sat for a long while upon the sled. No need to get up. He knew what had happened. The two dogs crouched and trembled at his feet.

At last, he passed a rope over his shoulder and pulled the sled along the trail with the dogs. At the first hint of darkness he made camp.

But he could not sleep that night. Before his eyes closed, the wolves had drawn too near for safety. Henry kept the fire blazing. It was the only thing that kept him from their hungry fangs. His two dogs stayed close to him, one on each side.

In the morning, the man was tired and wide-eyed from lack of sleep. He cooked breakfast in the darkness. After daylight, the wolves moved back. Then Henry chopped down saplings and built a deck high up between two trees. Using sled lashings, he hoisted the coffin up on top.

"They got Bill, an' they may get me, but they'll never get you," he said to the dead body.

Then he started off. The wolves were now following in the open. They trotted lazily behind, their red tongues hanging out.

At midday, Henry stopped and chopped a large supply of firewood.

With night came horror. The starving wolves were growing bolder. And Henry was suffering from lack of sleep. He dozed, crouching by the fire, wrapped in blankets. The axe lay between his knees, and the dogs stayed close against him.

Once, he came out of a doze to see the red-colored she-wolf not more than six feet away. She took no notice of the two dogs. She was looking at the man. She licked her chops.

He reached for a burning stick. But even as he reached, she sprang back. He knew that she was used to having things thrown at her.

All night, with burning sticks, he fought off the hungry pack. Morning came, but for the first time the wolves stayed in a circle about him in the light of day. The moment he left the protection of the fire, the boldest wolf leaped for him—but leaped short and sprang back, snapping his jaws. The rest of the pack was now up. The man threw fiery

sticks right and left to drive them back to a safe distance. Even in the daylight he did not dare leave the fire to chop fresh wood.

The night was the same as the night before, except that the man was even sleepier. Even the snarling of the dogs could not keep him awake. Once, after drifting off, he awoke with a start. The she-wolf was less than a yard from him. He thrust a burning stick into her snarling mouth. She sprang away, yelling with pain.

Before long, the man's eyes closed again. He dreamed. He dreamed he was safe inside Fort McGurry. It was warm and comfortable. Then, suddenly, wolves were howling at the fort gates. And then, in his dream, there was a crash. The door burst open. Wolves filled the room, leaping straight for him. And the howling—the loud howling—it was so clear—

And then he awoke to find the howling real. The wolves were rushing in—and were upon him! Without thinking, he leaped into the fire. Then began a firefight. His mittens protected his hands, and he scooped live coals into the air in every direction. The campfire looked like a volcano.

His face was blistering. His eyebrows and lashes were singed off. The heat was burning through his moccasins. With a flaming stick in each hand, he sprang to the edge of the fire. His two dogs were missing, and he well knew that they had been taken.

"You ain't got me yet!" he cried, shaking a fist at the snarling pack.

He set to work on a new idea. He pulled the fire out into a large circle, and crouched within the

circle of coals. The pack came curiously to the rim of the fire to see what had become of him. Then the she-wolf sat down, pointed her nose to a star, and began to howl. One by one the wolves joined her in the hunger cry.

Dawn came, and daylight. The fire was burning low. The fuel had run out. The man sat down. His shoulders drooped and his head fell to his knees. He had given up the struggle.

"I guess you can come an' get me any time," he mumbled. "Anyway, I'm goin' to sleep."

Once he awakened and he saw the she-wolf gazing at him.

Again he awakened, a little later, though it seemed hours to him. A mysterious change had taken place. The wolves were gone!

There were cries of men, and four sleds pulled in. Half a dozen men rushed to the man crouched inside the dying circle of fire.

"Red she-wolf…" he mumbled. "First she ate the dog food… Then she ate the dogs… An' after that she ate Bill…"

"Where's Lord Alfred?" one man yelled.

Bill shook his head. "No, she didn't eat him… He's roostin' in a tree in his box. Say, you lemme alone. I'm too tired. Goo'night, everybody."

His eyes fluttered and went shut. The men eased him down upon the blankets as his snores rose on the frosty air.

But there was another sound, far and faint in the distance. It was the cry of the hungry wolf pack as it took to the trail of other meat.

CHAPTER THREE

The Battle of the Fangs

It was the she-wolf who first heard the sounds of men's voices. And it was the she-wolf who was first to spring away from Henry and run into the darkness at the sound of his rescue.

Leading the pack was a large gray wolf. The she-wolf ran beside him. On her other side ran a thin old wolf, grizzled and marked with battle scars. He ran always on her right side, for his left eye was blind. At the back limped the weak members, the very young and the very old. At the front were the strongest.

Tired and starving, they ran on—day and night—over a frozen, dead world. No life stirred.

Finally, they came upon a bull moose. Here was meat and life, with no fires to guard it. The struggle was fierce, but the moose was brought down, and there was food in plenty. The wolves ate their fill. There was now resting and sleeping. The famine was over. The wolves were now in the world of life and game.

There came a day when the wolf pack split. The she-wolf, the young leader on her left, and the one-eyed elder on her right, led half the pack to the east. Each day, wolves left this group, until only four were left—the she-wolf, the young leader, the one-eyed one, and an eager three-year-old male.

The three-year-old grew daring. He attacked the one-eyed elder on his blind side. The third wolf joined the elder. Together, they attacked the three-year-old. Forgotten were the days when they had hunted together, and the hunger they had suffered. The time for mating was at hand.

The she-wolf, the cause of it all, sat down and watched as the two older wolves killed the three-year-old. But it was not over. When the young leader stopped to lick his wounds, the old one-eyed leader saw his chance. He leaped and his teeth tore at the younger leader's throat.

Bleeding and coughing, the young leader sprang at the elder and fought while life faded from him. Finally, the young leader lay in the snow and moved no more.

The days passed by, and One Eye and the she-wolf kept together, alone, hunting, killing, and eating their meat together. They did not remain in one place, but traveled across country until they came to the Mackenzie River.

There, one moonlit night, One Eye suddenly halted. The she-wolf trotted on, unalarmed. To their ears came the sounds of dogs scuffling, the rough cries of men, the voices of scolding women, and once the high cry of a child. And to their nostrils came the many smells of an Indian camp. One Eye did not know these sounds and these smells. But the she-wolf knew them well.

Old One Eye started slowly to go. The she-wolf turned and touched his neck with her muzzle. She wanted them to join the Indian camp. She felt an urge to go forward, to be in closer to that fire, to be squabbling with the dogs, and dodging the stumbling feet of men.

Eventually, One Eye was able to make her follow him—away from the camp.

As they traveled, they came upon a fresh rabbit trail. Both noses went down. One Eye caught sight of a white form on the white snow. He raced ahead after the fleeing animal. Leap by leap he gained. One leap more and it would be his. But that leap was never made. High in the air—and straight up—soared the white form. The snowshoe rabbit danced above him, struggling in the air, never to return to the ground.

One Eye sprang back with a snort of sudden fright. He crouched in the snow and snarled up at this thing he did not understand. But the she-wolf thrust coolly past him. She sprang for the dancing rabbit, but missed. She made another failed leap, and another.

One Eye watched her. He now made a mighty spring upward himself. His teeth closed upon the rabbit, and he pulled it back to earth. But at the same time there was a crackling movement beside him. A young spruce sapling was bending down above him to strike him! His jaws let go of the rabbit, and he leaped backward to escape this strange danger. The sapling snapped upright—and the rabbit soared into the air again.

The she-wolf was angry. She lunged at One Eye, then sat down in the snow. Old One Eye was now more afraid of his mate than the mysterious bending sapling. He again sprang for the rabbit. As he sank back with it between his teeth, he kept his eye on the sapling. As before, it followed him to earth. He crouched, waiting for the blow. But the blow did not come. The sapling remained bent above him.

The she-wolf took the rabbit from him, and while the sapling swayed above her she calmly gnawed the rabbit loose. At once the sapling shot up—and after that gave no more trouble. One Eye and the she-wolf ate the rabbit body that the strange sapling had caught for them.

There were other trails where rabbits were hanging in the air. Following the she-wolf's wise ways, One Eye soon learned the method of robbing snares. This was to serve him well in the days to come.

CHAPTER FOUR

Five Cubs to Feed

For two days the she-wolf and One Eye hung about the Indian camp. One morning, the air popped with the sound of a rifle, and a bullet smashed against a tree several inches from One Eye's head. They left the camp, but did not go far.

The she-wolf was trotting wearily along a small, rocky, frozen stream when she came upon a high, overhanging bank. The spring storms and melting snows had worn out an area in the bank. In one place, this had made a small cave.

She paused at the mouth of the cave. She looked the wall over carefully. It was dry and cozy. She finally entered its narrow mouth.

One Eye was hungry. He lay down in the entrance and slept, but did not sleep well. He tried to persuade his mate to get up, but she only snarled at him. So he walked out alone into the bright sunshine. He went up the frozen bed of the stream. He was gone for hours, and he came back through the darkness hungrier than when he had started. He had found game, but had not caught it.

He paused at the mouth of the cave. Faint, strange sounds came from within. He crawled inside on his belly and was met by a warning snarl from the she-wolf. He curled up and slept in the entrance.

When morning light came, One Eye could see, snuggled against her body, five strange little bundles of life. He went back outside to hunt.

Five or six miles from the cave, the stream divided into two forks. One Eye took the left fork going off between the mountains, and came upon a fresh track. The footprint was large—larger than his. He turned back and took the right fork. Within half a mile, his quick ears caught the sound of a porcupine gnawing on a tree. One Eye approached carefully.

The porcupine rolled itself into a ball. In his youth, One Eye had sniffed too near a ball of quills such as this—and the tail had flicked out suddenly in his face. So he lay down, his nose a foot away. After a while, he arose and trotted on. In the afternoon he came upon a grouse. The bird made a startled rise, but One Eye struck it with his paw, and caught it as it fluttered across the snow.

He headed for the cave with the grouse in his mouth. Near the stream, he came upon more of the large tracks he had seen that morning. He slid his head around a corner of rock. There he saw the maker of the tracks—a large female lynx. She was crouching in front of the tight-rolled ball of quills. One Eye lay hidden in the snow.

Half an hour passed—an hour—and nothing happened. At last, the porcupine decided that its enemy had gone. In the instant it began to unroll, the lynx struck. Everything happened at once—the blow, the tail flick, the squeal from the porcupine, the big cat's squall when it was stuck full of quills. The porcupine flicked out its tail again, and again the big cat squalled. She brushed her nose with her paws, trying to remove the fiery darts. Then she sprang away, squalling with every leap.

One Eye ventured forth. The porcupine had begun to roll up in a ball again. But its muscles were badly ripped and it was bleeding. Its long teeth gave one final clash. Then all the quills drooped down. The porcupine's body relaxed and moved no more.

One Eye studied it for a moment. He took a careful grip of the tender belly with his teeth. He started off, partly carrying, partly dragging the porcupine. When he reached the grouse, he ate it. Then he again took up the porcupine and dragged it back to the hungry she-wolf with her five cubs.

When he dragged the meat into the cave, the she-wolf looked it over. Then she turned her muzzle to One Eye and lightly licked him on the neck. But the next instant, she was warning him away from the cubs with a snarl.

CHAPTER FIVE

The Gray Cub

He was different from his brothers and sisters. Their hair had some of the reddish color of their mother, the she-wolf. He was the only one who looked like his father. He was the one little gray cub of the litter. He had mostly slept the first month of his life, but now he stayed awake more. His eyes had been open for a week. He was coming to learn his world quite well.

He was a fierce little cub. So were his brothers and sisters. It was to be expected. He came from a breed of meat-killers and meat-eaters. His father and mother lived upon meat. He had lived on milk for a month, but now was ready for meat.

He grew faster than his two brothers and two sisters. He was the first to learn the trick of rolling a fellow cub over. He was the first to grip another cub by the ear. And he certainly caused the mother the most trouble in keeping her cubs from the mouth of the cave.

Like most creatures of the Wild, he learned what it was like to go hungry. There came a time when there was no more meat, and the mother wolf could no longer make milk. At first, the cubs whimpered and cried—but mostly they slept. In time, only one sister and the gray cub lived. But the sister no longer lifted her head nor moved about. Food finally came, but too late for her.

Then there came a time when the gray cub no longer saw his father. The she-wolf knew why One Eye never came back, but had no way to explain that to the gray cub. When she had gone hunting for meat, she had followed a day-old trail of One Eye. And she had found him—and the signs of a battle with a lynx. The lynx had won. Before she went away, the she-wolf followed the tracks to the lynx's den. The signs told her that the lynx was inside with kittens. The she-wolf had not dared to go in.

By the time his mother began leaving the cave to hunt, the cub had learned about fear. He knew he must never go to the white wall of the cave where light shone in. When his mother was away, he slept most of the time. While he was awake he kept very quiet, with no whimpering.

Once, lying awake, he heard a strange sound. He did not know that it was a wolverine, standing outside, sniffing at the cave. The cub only knew that the sniff was strange and unknown. The cub lay still and silent—frozen with fear. When his mother came back, she growled as she smelled the wolverine's track. She bounded into the cave and licked and nuzzled her cub.

Fear kept the cub away from the white wall of light. But as the cub grew, his courage also grew. A wolf cub must know fear, but he must also grow—and learn—and put aside that fear so that he can explore his world. And so, one day the cub's fear was put aside by the rush of life. He stumbled and sprawled toward the white wall.

It was confusing to him. Fear told him to stay back. Something else drove him on. Soon he was at the mouth of the cave. He crouched down and gazed out on the world beyond the wall.

The wall opened out into a great light. Outside he saw things strange to his eyes. Trees. A stream. Huge mountains. And a blue sky high above that. The cub's hair stood on end. He wrinkled his lip and was ready to snarl at whatever came at him.

Nothing happened. He kept looking out, and forgot to snarl. Also, he forgot to be afraid, and he became curious.

Now, the gray cub had lived all his days on a flat floor. He had never been hurt in a fall. So he stepped boldly out upon the air. He fell forward from the cave onto his nose. Fear came back to him! He ki-yi'd like a frightened puppy as he rolled over and over and came to a stop at the bottom of the slope.

He sat up and looked about—and his curiosity returned. He inspected the grass, the plants, and a dead trunk of a pine tree. A squirrel hopped over and gave him a great fright. He snarled, and the squirrel ran for the pine tree.

Now the cub felt brave! When a moosebird rudely hopped up to him, the cub reached out at it with a playful paw. But the bird gave the cub a sharp peck on his nose that made him yelp. The bird quickly flew away.

He traveled very clumsily, but with every mishap he was learning. He was learning about the world and how to get around in it. He figured out that there were live things that moved, and not-alive things that did not move. He watched out for the live things.

The cub was born to be a hunter of meat, although he did not know it. He happened upon meat just outside his own cave door on this first adventure beyond the wall of white. It was by luck that he tripped and fell into the hidden grouse nest and found himself in a nest with seven chicks.

They made noises, and at first he was frightened. Then he placed his paw on one. He smelled it. He picked it up in his mouth. His jaws closed together. The taste of it was good. So he ate the grouse. Soon he had eaten the whole brood. The mother grouse arrived in a fury and he hid his head between his paws and yelped. Then he became angry. He sank his tiny teeth into one of her wings and pulled her into the open. The grouse struggled against the cub, but the cub was just doing what he was made for—killing meat and battling to kill it.

After a time, the bird stopped struggling. The cub still held her by the wing, and they lay on the ground and looked at each other. He tried to growl ferociously. She pecked on his nose. He winced—and began to whimper. He tried to back away, but he still held the grouse. A rain of pecks followed. The cub released the bird, then turned tail and scampered off. Once more, a fear of this unknown world rushed upon him. He shrank back into the shelter of a bush. Just then he felt a breeze of air fan him. A large, winged body swept silently past. A hawk, diving down out of the blue, had barely missed him.

It was a long time before the cub left his shelter and explored the stream. Not knowing better, he stepped boldly out onto the water—and went down! He came to the surface, and the sweet air rushed into his open mouth. He began to swim naturally. The near bank was only a yard away, but he had come up with his back to it. The first thing he saw was the opposite bank. Midway across, the current picked up the cub and swept him downstream. The quiet water became suddenly angry. Sometimes he was under, sometimes on top, sometimes smashing against the rocks.

Below the rapids was a pool of calm water. Here the water gently carried him toward the bank. He frantically crawled clear of the water. As he was scrambling between some bushes, he saw a flash of yellow. A long, lean weasel was leaping swiftly away from him. Then, at his feet, he saw a very small thing, only several inches long. It was a young weasel that had gone out adventuring, just like himself. The cub turned it over with his paw. Suddenly, yellow flashed again before his eyes! At the same instant he felt the sharp teeth of the mother weasel cut into his flesh. While he yelped, he saw the mother weasel grab her young one and disappear with it into the thicket.

The cub was still whimpering when the mother weasel returned. She came closer—and then her teeth were at his throat! The gray cub would have died—and there would have been no story to write about him—had the she-wolf not come bounding through the bushes. The weasel let go of the cub and flashed at the she-wolf's throat. It missed, catching hold on the jaw instead. The she-wolf whipped her head, flinging the weasel high in the air. And, still in the air, the she-wolf's jaws closed on the lean, yellow body.

The cub rested for two days, and then went out again. But on this trip he did not get lost. When he grew tired, he made his way back to the cave, and slept. Everyday after this, he made his way out and explored a wider area.

He grew and learned quickly. He learned when to be bold, and when to be cautious. The chatter of the squirrels no longer frightened him. But the shadow of the hawk sent him crouching into the nearest thicket.

The cub respected his mother. She could get meat, and she always brought him his share. She was unafraid of things. She had experience and knowledge, and to the cub this was power.

But meat became scarce again, and hunger and famine returned. The she-wolf ran herself thin hunting for meat. She rarely slept anymore in the cave. She spent most of her time on the meat-trail—and rarely found meat. This famine was not a long one, but it was hard while it lasted. The mother could no longer make milk for the cub, and she had no meat to bring him. The cub tried to chase down squirrels and dig mice out of their burrows. But he did not succeed. He crawled off to whimper out of hunger.

Finally, one day the she-wolf brought home meat. It was strange meat, different from any she had ever brought before. It was a lynx kitten, partly grown, like the cub, but not so large. And it was all for him. His mother had already eaten another lynx kitten. The cub did not know that this would put them in danger. He only knew that he was hungry—and here was meat. He ate and grew happier with every mouthful.

After eating, the cub fell asleep against his mother's side. Her snarling woke him. The cub looked up and saw, crouching in the entrance of the cave, the lynx mother.

The lynx tried to rush into the den, but the she-wolf sprang upon her. There was a tremendous snarling and spitting and screeching.

Once, the cub sprang in and sank his teeth into the hind-leg of the lynx. The next moment, the two mothers separated and the lynx lashed out at the cub, but that did not stop him. At the end of the battle, the cub was again clinging to a hind-leg and growling between his teeth.

The lynx mother was dead, but the she-wolf had been greatly injured. For more than a day she lay still. For a week she never left the cave,

except for water, and she moved slowly and painfully. At the end of that time they had finished eating the lynx. The she-wolf's wounds had healed enough for her to hunt again.

The cub began to hunt with his mother. He saw much of the killing and began to play his part in it. And he learned: *Life lived on life.* There were the eaters and the eaten. The law was: *Eat or be eaten.*

The world was full of surprise, and the cub learned to obey the laws of nature. The stir of life was in him. His muscles grew stronger. Running down meat was a thrill. Battles were pleasures. It was a joy to have a full stomach and doze lazily in the sunshine. This was all a part of life. He was very much alive, very happy, and very proud of himself.

CHAPTER SIX

The Makers of Fire

The cub came upon them suddenly. He had left the cave and run down to the stream to drink. He was trotting past the trees, and in one instant he saw and smelt. Before him were five live things he had never seen before. They did not move, but sat there on their haunches, silent. Nor did the cub move. He was in awe. He had never seen man, but he sensed their mastery and power.

One of the Indians arose and walked over to him. The cub cowered to the ground. As the Indian reached out a hand, the cub bared his fangs. The hand paused and the man laughed. *"Wabam wabisca ip pit tah."* ("Look! The white fangs!")

The other Indians laughed loudly, and urged the man to pick up the cub. As the hand came down, the cub's teeth sank into it. The next moment, the cub received a slap alongside the head that knocked him over on his side. He sat up on his haunches and ki-yi'd.

The four Indians laughed more loudly. Even the man who had been bitten began to laugh. Then the cub heard something, and knew what it was. He gave a last, long wail, and waited for the coming of his mother.

She bounded in amongst them, snarling as she ran. He bounded to meet her, while the man-animals quickly stepped back.

Then a cry went up from one of the men:

"Kiche!"

The cub felt his mother wilting at the sound. The she-wolf, the fearless one, crouched down till her belly touched the ground. She whimpered, wagged her tail, and made signs of peace. The men surrounded her, and felt her, and petted her.

"It is a year, Gray Beaver, since Kiche ran away," spoke an Indian.

"Yes—the year of the famine. There was no meat for the dogs. She is part wolf, so she left to live with the wolves. This be the sign of it," Gray Beaver answered. He laid his hand on the cub. The cub snarled a little at the touch of the hand.

"There is in him little dog and much wolf," Gray Beaver went on. "His fangs be white, and White Fang shall be his name."

White Fang watched as the man-animal tied a string of rawhide around his mother's throat. Then the man-animal led her to a small pine tree, where he tied the other end of the string. White Fang followed and lay down beside her. Another man-animal reached down to pet White Fang. White Fang snarled, but soon gave way as the hand rolled him over, rubbed his belly playfully, and tickled behind his ears. Then the man left him alone and went away. All fear had died out of White Fang.

After a time, White Fang heard new noises coming. He knew them at once for man-animal noises. A few minutes later the whole tribe trailed in—more men and many women and children, all carrying heavy camp equipment. Also there were many dogs and part-grown puppies. The grown dogs carried bags of thirty to forty pounds on their backs, fastened underneath.

White Fang had never seen dogs before. They were like his own kind, but somehow different. Suddenly, they attacked! White Fang could hear the snarl of Kiche as she fought for him. He could hear the cries of the man-animals, the sound of clubs striking upon bodies, and the yelps of pain from the dogs.

Within a few seconds he was on his feet again. He could now see the man-animals driving back the dogs with clubs and stones, saving him from the savage teeth of his kind that somehow was not his kind.

So much was new to White Fang. These man-animals who had a power—like gods. This new pack of animals that treated him cruelly. Before, he had only known One Eye, his mother, and himself. And now he resented that these, his kind, had tried to destroy him. He resented his mother being tied. This kept her away from him, and he was still in need of his mother's side. He no longer was free. And he did not like it.

The Indians arose and went on their march. A boy took the end of the rope and led Kiche. White Fang followed. They went down the valley to where the stream met the Mackenzie River.

Here, there were canoes stored on poles high in the air, and fish-racks for the drying of fish. The men set up the camp and built great tepees.

White Fang's mother was tied to a peg and he strayed away from her. A part-grown puppy came toward him slowly. The puppy's name, as White Fang later heard him called, was Lip-lip. White Fang prepared to meet him in friendly spirit. But suddenly, with remarkable swiftness, Lip-lip leaped in. Three times, four times, and half a dozen times, his sharp little teeth scored on the newcomer. Yelping in shame, White Fang fled to the side of his mother. Kiche licked him tenderly.

Before long, White Fang's curiosity returned, and he was venturing forth again. Gray Beaver was squatting and doing something with sticks and dry moss on the ground. White Fang came near to him and watched. He saw a strange thing like mist arise from the sticks beneath Gray Beaver's hands. He crawled several steps forward until his nose touched the flame. At the same instant his little tongue went out to it.

He scrambled backward, bursting in ki-yi's. Gray Beaver laughed loudly, and slapped his thighs. Soon everybody was laughing!

It was the worst hurt he had ever known. His nose and tongue were scorched. He cried hopelessly as the men laughed. And then the shame came to him. He now knew laughter and what it meant. And he felt shame that the man-animals were laughing at him. He turned and fled, not from the hurt of the fire, but from the laughter that sank even deeper. He fled to Kiche, the one creature in the world who was not laughing at him.

Night came, and White Fang lay by his mother's side. His nose and tongue still hurt. But worse than this, he was homesick. The only life he had known was gone.

He did not understand these man-animals. They held powers he did not hold. They could make dead things—stones and sticks—obey them. They could make sun-colored life spring from wood and moss. They were fire-makers! They were gods!

CHAPTER SEVEN

Life at Camp

While Kiche was tied by the stick, White Fang ran about the camp. He came to know the ways of the man-animals and their god-like powers. When they walked, he got out of their way. When they called, he came. When they were angry, he crouched down. When they commanded him to go, he obeyed. He learned about clubs and flying stones and stinging lashes of whips. He belonged to them as all dogs belonged to them.

But there were days when he crept to the edge of the forest and stood and listened to something calling him far and away. Yet always he returned, to whimper softly at Kiche's side.

The curse of his life was Lip-lip. He was a bully—larger, older, and stronger than White Fang. Lip-lip became a nightmare to him. Whenever White Fang slipped away from his mother, Lip-lip appeared. He trailed at White Fang's heels, snarling, picking on him. He would not allow White Fang to play with the other puppies at camp. He waited until no man-animals were around. Then he would spring upon White Fang and force a fight. Lip-lip always won.

Still, White Fang did not lose his spirit. Instead, he became more savage. He lost his playful, puppyish ways. He became more cunning in order to survive at camp. Lip-lip kept White Fang from his share of food, so White Fang became a clever thief. He learned to sneak about camp, to know what was going on everywhere, and to avoid Lip-lip.

The day came when Gray Beaver untied Kiche from the stick. White Fang was delighted with his mother's freedom. He walked with her joyfully about the camp. As long as he remained close by her side, Lip-lip kept his distance.

Later that day, White Fang led his mother, and they strayed off to the edge of the woods.

The stream, the cave, and the quiet forest were calling to him, and he wanted her to come. He ran on a few steps, stopped, and looked back. She had not moved. He whined. She only turned her head and gazed back at the camp.

There was something calling to him out there in the open. His mother heard it, too. But she heard also that other and louder call, the call of the fire and of man.

Kiche turned and slowly trotted back toward camp. White Fang whimpered. He was only a part-grown puppy. For him, there was still something stronger than the call of man or of the Wild. This was the call of his mother. So he arose and trotted sadly back to camp.

But White Fang's time with his mother was short. Gray Beaver was in debt to Three Eagles, who was going away on a trip up the Mackenzie River. Gray Beaver gave him a strip of scarlet cloth, a bearskin, and Kiche to pay the debt. White Fang saw his mother taken aboard Three Eagles' canoe, and tried to follow her. A blow from Three Eagles knocked him backward to the land. The canoe shoved off. He sprang into the water and swam after her!

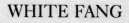

Gray Beaver angrily came after White Fang in a canoe. He reached down and, by the nape of the neck, lifted him clear of the water. He threw him into the bottom of the canoe and gave him a beating until White Fang could no longer stand.

When the canoe touched the shore, Gray Beaver flung White Fang, whimpering, onto the rocks. Lip-lip now rushed upon him. White Fang was too helpless to defend himself. He would have been badly hurt had Gray Beaver not kicked at Lip-lip. And so White Fang learned that only the gods had the right to punish.

That night, White Fang cried for his mother. Gray Beaver, awakened by White Fang's cries, beat him again. He cried no more around the gods. But sometimes, he would stray to the edge of the woods by himself and cry out with loud whimperings. For now he was alone.

He could have run back to the Wild, but the memory of his mother held him to camp. Sometimes Three Eagles visited the camp with Kiche. So White Fang stayed—always waiting for her. Before long, he had learned how to get along with Gray Beaver. The man-animal never petted him, but he fed him and defended him.

Lip-lip, however, kept bullying him. The young dogs followed Lip-lip's lead. White Fang could whip many of them one-on-one, but a fight was a signal for all the young dogs in camp to come running. When White Fang did win, the man-animals beat him. This made White Fang more ferocious. He became an outcast, and a sneak and a troublemaker. But he learned how to take care of himself in a mass fight. He became cat-like in his ability to stay on his feet. Grown dogs could hurtle him backward, but he always went with his legs under him and his feet to the earth, ready to spring forward or away.

White Fang learned to attack quickly. If he could take a dog by surprise, the dog was already half-whipped.

The pack would not allow White Fang to run with them. And White Fang would attack any dog that was alone. The young dogs, except for Lip-lip, became afraid to run by themselves. But the pack would go after White Fang and hunt him as he ran—and lost them—through the woods.

In time, man and dog both hated White Fang. The tooth of every dog was against him, the hand of every man. He was alert for any attack.

He was hated by his own kind and mankind. But he learned how to survive. He learned to obey the strong and to go after the weak. Gray Beaver was the strong. Therefore White Fang obeyed him. But any dog younger or smaller than himself was weak, a thing to be destroyed. He became quicker than the other dogs, swifter of foot, craftier, deadlier, more lean with iron-like muscle. He was more cruel, more ferocious, and more intelligent. He had to become all these things, or he would not have survived in the world in which he found himself.

CHAPTER EIGHT

Changes and New Laws

In the fall, the summer camp was taken down. The tribe was preparing to go off to the fall hunting grounds. White Fang watched it all. When the tepees began to come down and the canoes were loading at the bank, he understood. He crawled into the dense thicket and waited.

He heard Gray Beaver calling him by name, but he did not move. The voices died away and darkness came. For a while he played among the trees, enjoying his freedom. Then, suddenly, he was aware of loneliness. He became frightened. He felt cold. Here was no warm side of a tepee against which to snuggle. Here was no meat.

White Fang had forgotten how to take care of himself. A panic seized him, and he ran madly toward the village. He passed out of the forest and into the moonlit open. But no village greeted his eyes. The man-animals had moved on—without him.

He slunk sadly through the deserted camp, smelling the rubbish heaps. He would have been glad just to hear the rattle of stones being flung his way. He would have been happy to see Gray Beaver. He longed to see Lip-lip and the whole snarling pack again.

He came to where Gray Beaver's tepee had stood. There he sat down. He pointed his nose at the moon. With a heart-broken cry, filled with loneliness and grief for Kiche, he howled a long wolf-howl. It was his first howl.

When daylight came, he plunged back into the forest to search for the trail of the gods. All day he ran. He did not rest. By the middle of the second day, he had been running for thirty hours. He had not eaten in forty hours, and he was weak with hunger. His handsome coat was draggled. His feet were bruised and bleeding. He had begun to limp. To make it worse, snow began to fall.

Night had fallen when White Fang limped across a fresh-smelling trail in the snow. He knew it immediately for what it was! He hurried along the trail and came into the new camp. There was Gray Beaver, crouching by the fire.

White Fang was afraid of the beating he'd get from Gray Beaver. But he also knew how safe and warm he would be near his fire once more— even with the other hated dogs. White Fang crawled slowly toward Gray Beaver, waiting for his punishment.

Gray Beaver put out his hand—but he did not hit White Fang. Instead, he offered him a piece of fresh meat. After that, White Fang lay at Gray Beaver's feet, gazing at the fire that warmed him.

In December, Gray Beaver went on a journey up the Mackenzie River. Mit-sah and Kloo-kooch—Gray Beaver's son and wife—went with him. Gray Beaver drove one sled himself. Mit-sah drove a smaller sled with a team of seven puppies. Most were nine and ten months old, but White Fang was only eight months old.

Mit-sah looked like his father, and had much of his father's wisdom. He was aware that Lip-lip bullied White Fang, but Lip-lip had been another man's dog. His father had done some trading, and now Lip-lip was Mit-sah's dog. He placed Lip-lip at the end of the longest rope. This made Lip-lip the leader. But instead of being bully and master of the pack, Lip-lip now found himself hated by the pack. The moment the sled started, the team took after Lip-lip in a chase that lasted the whole day. Even though Lip-lip was the head dog, he was no longer "leader" among the other puppies.

White Fang enjoyed the work. He worked hard, learned discipline, and was obedient. Still, he stayed to himself. He had never learned to play. Since Lip-lip no longer ruled the others, White Fang could have become leader of the pack. But he just wanted to be left alone. They knew to get out of his way when he came along. Even the boldest of them would never dare to rob him of his meat. In fact, they quickly ate their own meat, for fear that he would take it away from them. White Fang knew the law well:

Oppress the Weak. Obey the Strong.

The months passed by. White Fang grew stronger with the long hours on the trail and the steady toil at the sled. He had come to know the world as a fierce and brutal place. He had no love for Gray Beaver. He respected him and obeyed him, but he felt no love. If Gray Beaver had given him a kind word, or a gentle touch, White Fang might have felt something deeper for this god. But Gray Beaver did not pet him nor speak kind words. It was not his way.

So White Fang knew nothing of the kindness a man's hand might offer. Besides, he did not like the hands of the man-animals. He did not trust them. It was true they sometimes gave him meat, but more often they gave hurt. Hands were things to keep away from. They hurled stones, held clubs and sticks and whips. In strange villages that they came to, White Fang stayed away from hands—especially those of children, who could pinch and hurt.

In a village at the Great Lake, White Fang learned a new law: *Never bite one of the gods*. A boy was chopping frozen moose-meat. White Fang stopped and began to eat the small pieces that flew off into the snow. The boy laid down his axe,

took up a club, and chased White Fang between two tepees. He trapped White Fang against a high earth bank. White Fang was furious. He had done no wrong! One thing led to the next, and the boy somehow found himself on his back. His club-hand was bleeding where White Fang had bitten him. Then White Fang knew he had done wrong.

White Fang fled away to Gray Beaver and crouched behind his legs. When the boy's family came, they demanded that the dog be punished. But Gray Beaver, Mit-sah, and Kloo-kooch defended him. White Fang had learned that to bite a god was wrong—but that not all gods were allowed to punish him.

Before the day was out, White Fang learned a new law: *Protect your own*. Mit-sah was gathering firewood in the forest when he was attacked by a gang of boys. They were led by the boy who had been bitten. White Fang looked on. One of his own gods was being hurt! Anger filled him and he jumped to Mit-sah's defense. Five minutes later, the gang of boys had fled. When Mit-sah told his story in camp, Gray Beaver ordered meat to be given to White Fang. White Fang knew he was being rewarded for his protection of the pack.

In the days that followed, White Fang learned more about protecting his pack and his pack's property. Gray Beaver trained him to protect them from thieves. He became a guard dog—and no man and no other dog could get past him. In return, White Fang was rewarded with food and the warmth of the fire.

The bond between man and dog grew stronger as the months went by. White Fang did his duty to protect his own. He felt awe and respect for his gods. But he did not feel love. He did not know what love was. The memory of his mother, Kiche, slowly left him. His bond to the man-animals became stronger than a need for freedom—and his old home in the Wild.

CHAPTER NINE

The Famine

In April, Gray Beaver returned to the summer village. White Fang was now a year old. Though still not fully grown, he was larger than the others his age—except for Lip-lip. And he was intelligent. His strong build came from his wolf father, and his mental strength from his half-dog mother.

The man-animals cut up a large moose, giving parts to the dogs. White Fang got a hoof and part of the shinbone with quite a bit of meat attached. He was eating his prize when Baseek, an old dog, rushed in upon him. White Fang slashed back at him, and Baseek stepped back in surprise. The meaty shinbone lay between them.

Baseek bristled fiercely and snarled across the shinbone. White Fang felt small, and looked for a way to escape. But then Baseek made his mistake. He still thought of White Fang as just a pup and himself as the strong bully. He stepped forward to the meat.

This was too much for White Fang. He could not stand by while another took what belonged to him. He struck without warning and Baseek was knocked off his feet. His throat was bitten. His ear ripped. His shoulder torn. The swiftness of it was bewildering.

The situation was now reversed. White Fang stood over the shinbone and snarled at Baseek. Baseek calmly retreated.

White Fang had stood his ground against a full-grown dog. He now walked proudly among the dogs. The older dogs quickly learned that if they left him alone, he left them alone.

In midsummer, White Fang was trotting along the edge of the village when he came upon Kiche. He paused and looked at her. He began to remember her, but she did not remember him. She lifted her lip in a snarl—and then the old memories rushed back to him. He bounded

toward her joyously, but she met him with sharp fangs. He did not understand. He backed slowly away, puzzled.

But it was not Kiche's fault. A wolf mother was not made to remember her cubs of a year or so before. So she did not remember White Fang. He was now a strange animal. She had a new litter of puppies to guard.

White Fang looked at Kiche licking one of her new puppies. There was no place for her in his life anymore. There was no place for him in hers. Kiche snarled once more at him, and White Fang walked away.

The months went by and White Fang grew stronger and heavier. He had only one weakness. He could not stand being laughed at. It so outraged him that for hours he would behave like a demon, racing about and attacking other dogs.

In the third year of his life, a great famine came to the Mackenzie Indians. In the summer the fish failed. In the winter the caribou and moose were scarce. The rabbits almost disappeared. Only the strong survived. The old and weak died of hunger. There was wailing in the village as all went hungry.

A few of the boldest and wisest dogs fled into the forest. There, in the end, they starved to death or were eaten by wolves.

In this time of misery, White Fang also stole away into the woods. Unlike the other dogs, he had learned the ways of the woods in his cubhood. He hunted out squirrels and wood mice, patiently and cunningly. He even robbed one of Gray Beaver's rabbit snares.

He journeyed over to the valley and stream where he had been born. Here, in the old cave, he came upon Kiche. She, too, had fled the camp and had given birth to more puppies. Only one puppy remained alive. White Fang looked in, then left and trotted on up the stream. He found the old hiding place of the lynx that he and his mother had fought long before. Here he settled down and rested for a day.

During the early summer, he met Lip-lip, who had also taken to the woods. Trotting in opposite directions around a high bluff, they each rounded a corner of rock and found themselves face to face. Lip-lip learned too late that small cubs soon grow up, and that they remember. White Fang left him dead by the stream.

One day, not long after, White Fang came to the edge of the forest. Here a narrow stretch of open land sloped down to the Mackenzie River. He paused to study the situation. Familiar sights, sounds, and scents called to him. It was the old village changed to a new place. And there was a smell in the air of fish. There was food. The famine was gone. He came out boldly from the forest and trotted straight to Gray Beaver's tepee. Gray Beaver was not there, but Kloo-kooch welcomed him with glad cries and fresh fish. He lay down to wait for Gray Beaver.

CHAPTER TEN

The Enemy of His Kind

With Lip-lip gone, Mit-sah made White Fang the new leader of the sled team. This made the dogs hate him. They hated him when Mit-sah gave him extra meat. They hated him because he seemed to receive special favors. And they hated him because he was always at the head of their team—fleeing just out of reach.

And White Fang hated them back. He hated being at the head of the yelling pack. He hated running away from the dogs he had defeated for the past three years. And if he turned upon them, Mit-sah would throw the stinging lash of the whip into his face.

White Fang could only slow down when Mit-sah cried out for the team to stop. At first this caused trouble for the other dogs. They would attack White Fang only to be hit with the whip by Mit-sah. So the dogs came to understand that when Mit-sah gave the order to stop, White Fang was to be let alone. But when White Fang stopped without orders, then they were allowed to spring upon him.

The dogs learned that it was best to keep together. White Fang was too terrible for any of them to face alone. He was too quick for them, too big, too wise. Unlike the other dogs, he still had the Wild in him. He was the enemy of his own kind. Gray Beaver could not help but admire and marvel at White Fang.

When White Fang was nearly five years old, Gray Beaver took him on another journey. In many of the villages along the way, White Fang attacked the strange dogs. They were ordinary dogs. They were not prepared for his swiftness. They growled, but White Fang wasted no time growling. He was at their throats before they knew what was happening. He was a skilled fighter. The dogs had no chance against him.

It was in the summer that White Fang and Gray Beaver arrived at Fort Yukon. Gray Beaver had crossed between the Mackenzie and the Yukon rivers in the late winter. He spent the spring hunting along the western Rockies. He waited for the ice to break up on the Porcupine River. Then he had built a canoe and paddled down that stream to meet the Yukon River just under the Arctic Circle. It was the summer of 1898. Thousands of gold-hunters were going up the Yukon. Some had even come from the other side of the world.

Here Gray Beaver stopped. A whisper of the gold rush had reached his ears. He had come with several bales of furs, mittens, and moccasins to trade. It was a good trip. He made more profit than he expected.

It was at Fort Yukon that White Fang saw his first white men. They had houses and a huge fort of logs. For the first few hours he was content with slinking around and watching them from a safe distance. The white men also watched White Fang with great curiosity. They pointed him out to one another. When they came near him, he showed his teeth and backed away.

Every two or three days, a steamboat stopped at the bank for several hours. The white men came off these steamers and went away on them again. White Fang was cautious with the white men, but not with their dogs. He was an enemy of all dogs. All he had to do, when the strange dogs came ashore, was to show himself. They rushed at him from off the ships out of instinct. But these dogs were soft and helpless. White Fang sprang to the side, confusing the dogs. In that moment he struck them on the shoulder, rolling them off their feet and going for the throat. The pack would rush in and finish killing the dog, while White Fang ran to safety.

It was then that the white men rushed in. White Fang would stand off at a little distance and look on, while stones, clubs, axes, and all sorts of weapons fell upon the other dogs. White Fang enjoyed it all. He did not love his own kind. He hated all dogs—those of the Indians, and those of the white men.

How could White Fang have turned out any other way? He had seen the first light of day in a lonely cave. He had fought his first fights in the Wild—with the grouse, the weasel, and the lynx.

His puppyhood had been made bitter by the bullying of Lip-lip and the whole puppy pack. If Lip-lip had never existed, White Fang might have grown up happily with the other puppies. He would have become more doglike, with more liking for dogs. If Gray Beaver had shown just a little love, White Fang might have turned out more trusting and kind. But these things had not been so. The world molded White Fang until he became what he was. He was unloving and ferocious. He was the enemy of all his kind.

CHAPTER ELEVEN

Beauty Smith

The few white men who lived in Fort Yukon had been there a long time. They made fun of the newcomers who arrived on the steamers and enjoyed seeing them make mistakes. And they enjoyed seeing the newcomers' dogs being "met" at the docks by White Fang and the other camp dogs. It was a sport to watch the dogs fight.

There was one man who particularly enjoyed the sport. He would come running at the first sound of a steamboat's whistle. When a soft newcomer's dog went down, he cried out with delight. He stayed until the last fight was over, and White Fang and the pack had scattered.

The other men called this man "Beauty" Smith. But he was anything but a beauty. He did the cooking for the other men in the fort, the dishwashing and the unpleasant work. And the men feared him. He was weak and cowardly—and this made him cruel and disliked.

Beauty Smith kept a sharp eye on White Fang. This was an animal he wanted to own. White Fang didn't like the man. He sensed evil in him.

White Fang was in Gray Beaver's camp when Beauty Smith first visited. Gray Beaver refused to sell the dog. He had grown rich with his trading and needed nothing. But Beauty Smith visited Gray Beaver's camp often, and hidden under his coat was always a bottle of whiskey. Each time he tried to buy White Fang, he shared his bottle. Gray Beaver started buying whiskey—and grew to crave the taste. It was not long before Gray Beaver's money was gone. Nothing remained but his thirst for whiskey. Beauty Smith talked with him again about the sale of White Fang. But this time the price offered was in bottles, not dollars, and Gray Beaver's ears were eager.

White Fang slunk into camp one evening, tired but content. But he had scarcely lain down when Gray Beaver staggered over to him. He tied a leather strap around his neck. An hour passed and Beauty Smith strode into camp and stood over White Fang. One hand began to come down upon the dog's head. White Fang's snarl grew tense and harsh. Suddenly he snapped, striking with his fangs like a snake. The hand was jerked back. Beauty Smith was frightened and angry. Gray Beaver clouted White Fang alongside the head, so that he lay down obediently.

Beauty Smith went away and returned with a stout club. Then Gray Beaver gave over the end of the strap, and Beauty Smith started to walk away. White Fang resisted. Gray Beaver hit him to make him follow. White Fang rushed forward, hurling himself upon Beauty. Beauty Smith did not jump away. He was expecting this. He swung the club smartly, sending White Fang to the ground. Gray Beaver laughed. Beauty Smith tightened the strap again, and White Fang crawled limply and dizzily to his feet. He did not rush a second time. He followed at Beauty Smith's heels, his tail between his legs, and snarling under his breath.

At the fort, Beauty Smith left him tied outside. In ten seconds, White Fang chewed through the leather and hurried back to Gray Beaver's camp.

Gray Beaver again put a leash on him, and in the morning turned him over to Beauty Smith, who gave him a beating. Club and whip were both used upon him. It was the worst beating White Fang had known in his life.

Beauty Smith enjoyed the task as he swung the whip and club, and listened to White Fang's helpless cries. For Beauty Smith was cruel in the way that cowards are cruel. They can't be men to men, but must be brutes to anything weaker than themselves.

After the beating, Beauty Smith dragged White Fang back to the fort and tied him to a stick. During the night, White Fang again chewed free and went back to Gray Beaver. But he was betrayed yet a third time. And this time he was beaten even more severely than before.

White Fang was dragged again to the fort and was now tied with a chain. After a few days, Gray Beaver left to return to the Mackenzie. White Fang remained on the Yukon. He now belonged to a man more than half mad and all brute.

White Fang was chained in a pen at the back of the fort. Here Beauty Smith teased and irritated him. The man discovered White Fang's hatred of laughter, and made it a point to trick him and then laugh at him.

White Fang had now become an enemy and hater of *all* things. He hated the chain around his neck. He hated the men who looked in at him through the slats of the pen. He hated the dogs that snarled at him. He hated the very wood of the pen that held him. And first, last, and most of all, he hated Beauty Smith.

But Beauty Smith had a purpose in all that he did. One day a number of men gathered about the pen. Beauty Smith entered, club in hand, and took the chain off White Fang's neck. White Fang tore around the inside of the pen. The men admired him. He was bigger than the average wolf. He was all muscle—ninety pounds of fighting fury.

The door of the pen was opened again. White Fang paused. Then a huge dog—a mastiff—was thrust inside, and the door was slammed shut. The mastiff sprung, but White Fang leaped in with a flash of fangs that ripped at the dog's neck.

The men outside shouted and applauded. Beauty Smith was delighted with White Fang's fighting ability. There was no hope for the mastiff from the start. In the end, the dead mastiff was dragged out by its owner. Then there was a payment of bets, and money clinked in Beauty Smith's hand.

White Fang came to look forward to when men gathered around his pen. It meant a fight. One day he fought three dogs in a row. Once he fought two dogs at once. He was always the victor.

In the fall of the year, Beauty Smith bought tickets for himself and White Fang on a steamboat bound up the Yukon. White Fang was known far and wide as "The Fighting Wolf." Men stared at him, poked sticks between the bars of his cage on the ship, and then laughed at him.

When the steamboat arrived at Dawson, White Fang went ashore. Men paid fifty cents in gold dust just to see "The Fighting Wolf." He was given no rest. Whenever he lay down to sleep, he was stirred up by a sharp stick—so that the audience might get its money's worth. He was kept in a rage most of the time, and was called the most fearsome of wild beasts.

When a fight was arranged, he was taken out of his cage at night and led off into the woods a few miles from town to avoid the police. He always won his matches. He was fast, he rushed in quickly, and he was experienced. He knew more about fighting than any dog that faced him. In time, no one would pit his dog against White Fang. Beauty drew a crowd when he had White Fang fight a wild wolf. Once, he tossed in a full-grown female lynx. White Fang fought for his life.

After the lynx, all fighting stopped for White Fang. There were no more animals to pit against him. So he remained on exhibition until spring, when Tim Keenan, a card-dealer, arrived in the land. With him came the first bulldog that had ever entered the Klondike. Everyone knew that this dog and White Fang would fight.

CHAPTER TWELVE

The Clinging Death

Beauty Smith slipped the chain from White Fang's neck and stepped back.

For once White Fang did not make an immediate attack. He had never seen such a dog before. Tim Keenan shoved the bulldog forward with a muttered, "Go to it." The dog waddled toward the center of the circle. He stopped and blinked at White Fang.

There were cries from the crowd of "Go to him, Cherokee!" "Eat him up!"

But Cherokee did not seem anxious to fight. He turned and blinked at the men and wagged his stump of a tail. He was not afraid—just lazy.

Tim Keenan stepped in and bent over the bulldog, giving him another shove forward. Then White Fang struck. A cry of startled admiration went up from the crowd.

The bulldog was bleeding behind one ear from a rip in his thick neck. He gave no sign of pain, did not even snarl, but turned and followed after White Fang. The bulldog's bowlegged, steady walk and White Fang's quickness excited the crowd. The men were making new bets. Again, and yet again, White Fang sprang in and got away untouched. Still the strange dog waddled after him.

White Fang was puzzled. He had never seen such a dog. It was soft and slow and gave no cry. White Fang could never get at the soft underside of the throat. The bulldog stood too short, and its huge jaws were in the way. Those same jaws were patiently waiting to get a grip on White Fang.

The time went by. White Fang dodged and danced about, striking again and again. The bulldog's ears had been torn, his neck and shoulders were slashed, and his very lips were cut and bleeding. Still he wagged his stumpy tail and blinked at the men. He was just waiting—waiting to get his own grip on White Fang's throat.

Time and again, White Fang tried to knock Cherokee off his feet. But Cherokee was too close to the ground. White Fang tried the trick once too often. One last time he drove in, but his own shoulder was high above Cherokee's. He struck, turned a half-somersault in the air, and went right over the bulldog's body. For the first time, men saw White Fang lose his footing. In that instant, Cherokee's teeth closed on his throat.

It was not a good grip. It was too low down toward the chest, but Cherokee held on. White Fang sprang to his feet and tore wildly around, trying to shake off the bulldog's body. It made him frantic, this clinging, dragging weight. Round and round he went, whirling and turning. The bulldog did little but keep his grip. He knew he was doing the right thing by holding on. The grip was the thing, and the grip he kept.

The bulldog pushed forward and rolled White Fang over on his back, still hanging on to his throat. Slowly it shifted his grip, moving up the throat. Bit by bit, whenever the chance offered, the bulldog slowly choked White Fang. There was no escaping the grip. White Fang could do nothing. The battle would soon be over.

Beauty Smith knew how to get White Fang riled. He took a step into the ring and pointed his finger at White Fang. Then he began to laugh. White Fang went wild with rage and gained his feet. Round and round, stumbling and falling, he fought against the clinging death. But at last he fell again. Shouts of applause went up. Cherokee responded by wagging the stump of his tail.

It was at this time that there came a jingle of bells. Everybody, except Beauty Smith, looked up in fear that the police were coming. Two men rode up with sleds and dogs. Seeing the crowd, the men stopped. The dog-musher wore a mustache. The taller, younger man was smooth-shaven.

White Fang had stopped struggling. He could get little air. When Beauty Smith saw White Fang's eyes beginning to glaze, he knew the fight was lost. He sprang upon White Fang in anger and began to kick him. At that moment, the tall, young newcomer forced his way through the crowd and sent his fist into Beauty's face. Beauty Smith seemed to lift into the air as he turned over backward and struck the snow. The newcomer's gray eyes flashed upon the crowd.

"You cowards!" he cried. "You beasts!"

Beauty Smith, the coward that he was, lay where he had fallen, making no effort to get up.

"Come on, Matt, lend a hand," the newcomer called to the dog-musher.

Both men bent over the dogs. Matt took hold of White Fang, ready to pull when the tall man could loosen Cherokee's jaws.

The crowd began to grow unruly. The tall man raised his head and glared at them.

"Won't some of you help?" he cried.

No help was offered.

"It's no use, Mr. Scott, you can't break 'em apart that way," Matt said. "You'll need a pry."

Scott tried to thrust the muzzle of his revolver between the bulldog's jaws to pry them open.

Tim Keenan strode into the ring. "Don't break them teeth, stranger."

"Then I'll break his neck," Scott answered.

He managed to get the muzzle in between the jaws on one side and out between the jaws on the other side. He pried gently and carefully, loosening the jaws a bit at a time.

Keenan stooped down and got a firm hold on Cherokee. The dogs were finally pulled apart, though the bulldog continued to struggle.

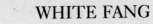

White Fang made a few attempts to get up. His legs were too weak, and he sank down into the snow. His eyes were half-closed. He looked like a dog that had been strangled to death.

Matt looked him over and said, "Just about done in, but he's breathin'."

"Matt, how much is a good sled dog worth?" Scott asked.

"Three hundred dollars."

"And how much for one that's all chewed up?"

"Half of that."

Scott turned to Beauty Smith. "I'm going to give you a hundred and fifty for him."

"I ain't a-sellin'," Beauty said.

"Oh, yes, you are," the other assured him. "The dog's mine."

"I know my rights," Beauty said fearfully.

"You lost your rights to own that dog. Are you going to take the money? Or do I have to hit you again?"

"All right," said Beauty Smith. "But I'm bein' robbed, and a man's got rights."

"Correct," Scott answered, passing the money over to him. "A man's got rights. But you're not a man. You're a beast."

Off to the side, Tim Keenan asked quietly, "Who *is* that mug?"

"Weedon Scott," someone whispered. "He's a mining expert. I'd steer clear of him. He's all hunky with the officials."

"I thought he must be somebody," Keenan said. "That's why I kept my hands off of him at the start."

CHAPTER THIRTEEN

Weedon Scott

"It's hopeless," said Weedon Scott. "It's a wolf and there's no taming it."

"He's been tamed a'ready," Matt said. "D'ye see them harness marks across the chest? He was a sled dog at one time. And he was probably a good sled dog."

"But we've had him two weeks," Scott said, "and if anything, he's wilder than ever."

"Turn 'im loose for a spell," Matt said. "Could be the cage makin' 'im crazy."

"Won't he run away?" Scott asked.

Matt shrugged his shoulders. "Only way to find out is find out."

Matt grabbed a club and went over to the chained animal. The dog-musher unsnapped the chain and stepped back.

White Fang couldn't believe he was free. He saw the younger man toss him a piece of meat. He sprang away, and studied it from a safe distance.

"Major! No!" Matt shouted, but too late.

Major, the lead sled dog, had made a spring for the meat. At the instant his jaws closed on it, White Fang's closed on Major's throat. Matt's foot kicked at White Fang. White Fang tore a gash out of Matt's leg, then jumped back.

"He got me, all right," Matt said, holding his leg.

"I told you it was hopeless, Matt. There's only one thing to do," Scott said. He drew his revolver. "We can't have him attacking people."

"But I had no right to kick 'im, Mr. Scott," Matt argued. "Give the poor devil a chance. Please don't shoot 'im. I know he can be petted. Look at 'im. He knows he done wrong."

Scott put away the revolver. White Fang lowered himself down into the snow.

"You're sure?" Scott asked.

"Yes, I'm sure. He was petted at sometime in his life, wasn't he? He was a sled dog."

Scott believed the dog-musher, and slowly reached out his hand. "Here, good boy."

But the dog-musher was mistaken. As Weedon Scott approached, White Fang snarled.

Scott sat down several feet away. He remained quiet and made no movement. White Fang's snarl slowly became a low growl that grew softer and softer. Then Scott spoke. At the first sound of the man's voice, the hair rose on White Fang's neck. The growl rushed back up in his throat. But Scott made no movement and went on talking calmly.

After a long time, Scott held out a small piece of meat. White Fang pricked up his ears and looked at it suspiciously.

Scott tossed the meat on the snow at White Fang's feet. He smelled the meat carefully, but kept his eyes on Scott. Then he slowly ate the meat. Scott offered him another piece of meat. White Fang would not take it from the hand. Again Scott tossed it to him. Scott did this a few times. But one time, Scott held onto the meat.

Bit by bit, White Fang approached the hand. A low growl rumbled in his throat. He ate the meat, and nothing happened. Piece by piece, he ate all the meat, and nothing happened.

Scott went on talking. And then, Scott reached forth his hand. White Fang snarled and bristled and flattened his ears. But he didn't snap or spring away. The hand touched the ends of his bristling hair. White Fang shrank down under it. He could not forget all the evil that had been done against him at the hands of men.

The hand lifted and came down again in a kind, patting movement. Scott talked softly, and his hand patted gently.

"Well, I'll be gosh-swoggled!" exclaimed Matt, coming out of the cabin. White Fang leaped back, snarling savagely at Matt.

Weedon Scott stood and walked over to White Fang. He talked quietly to him, then slowly put out his hand and rested it on White Fang's head.

"You may be a number one, tip-top mining expert, all right," Matt said, "but you're a wild animal tamer, too! When you was a boy you shoulda run off to join a circus."

It was the beginning of the end for White Fang. It was the ending of the old life ruled by hate. It was the beginning of a new life—with Weedon Scott. It was Weedon Scott's patience and love that changed White Fang.

Weedon Scott was determined to tame White Fang. Each day he made it a point to pet him. White Fang grew to like this petting, but he never outgrew his growling. However, it was now a growl of contentment, and Scott knew this.

White Fang had never known such kindness, and his *like* for Weedon Scott grew to *love*. He felt protective of this man who treated him fairly and gently. He prowled about the cabin while the sled dogs slept. He listened for any stranger. The first night-visitor to the cabin fought him off with a club until Scott came to the rescue. Eventually, White Fang learned to tell the difference between friend and enemy. He let any man alone who stepped loudly to the cabin door. But he attacked any man who went softly and secretly.

White Fang was changing. He no longer roamed the woods, or hid at the corner of the cabin. Instead, he would wait for hours on the cabin steps for a sight of Weedon Scott's face.

In the late spring, Scott suddenly disappeared. White Fang had never seen a suitcase before, so he did not know what it meant. That night he waited in the cold on the front step for his master to return. But Scott never came.

In the morning, Matt opened the door and stepped outside. White Fang gazed at him sadly. The days came and went, but never Weedon Scott. White Fang, who had never known sickness, became so sick that Matt finally brought him inside the cabin. He wrote a letter to Scott:

"That wolf won't eat.
Mebbe he is going to die."

It was as Matt had said. White Fang lay on the floor of the cabin near the stove—without interest in food, in Matt, nor in life. Matt talked gently to him, but it made no difference. White Fang just turned his dull eyes upon the man, and then dropped his head back on his forepaws.

One night, Matt was startled by a low whine from White Fang. He had got upon his feet, his ears cocked toward the door. A moment later, Matt heard a footstep. The door opened, and Weedon Scott stepped in. The two men shook hands. Then Scott looked around the room.

"Where's the wolf?" he asked.

Then he discovered him, standing where he had been lying, near the stove. He had not rushed forward in the manner of other dogs. He stood, watching and waiting.

"Look at 'im wag his tail!" Matt exclaimed.

Weedon Scott strode halfway across the room toward him, at the same time calling him. White Fang came to him, not with a great bound, yet quickly. As he drew near, his eyes took on a strange expression.

"He never looked at me that way all the time you was gone," Matt commented.

Weedon Scott did not hear. He was squatting down on his heels, face to face with White Fang, petting him and listening to him growl. White Fang suddenly thrust his head forward and nudged his way in between the master's arm and body. And here, hidden from view except for his ears, no longer growling, he continued to nudge and snuggle.

One night, Scott and Matt sat playing a game of cards before going to bed. A wild scream of fear came from outside.

"The wolf's nailed somebody," Matt said.

"Bring a light!" Scott sprang outside.

Matt followed with the lamp, and by its light they saw a man lying on his back in the snow. His arms were folded across his face and throat. He was shielding himself from White Fang's teeth.

Weedon Scott grabbed White Fang and dragged him back. Matt helped the man to his feet. As he arose, Matt saw the beastly face of Beauty Smith. Matt let go quickly, as if he had touched fire.

At the same moment, Matt shone the lamp on two objects lying in the snow—a steel dog-chain and a stout club. Weedon Scott saw and nodded. Not a word was spoken. Matt laid his hand on Beauty Smith's shoulder and turned him around toward the woods. Beauty Smith scurried off.

Weedon Scott patted White Fang.

"Tried to steal you, eh? And you wouldn't have it! Well, well, he made a mistake, didn't he?"

They never saw Beauty Smith again.

CHAPTER FOURTEEN

The Southland

"Listen to that, will you!" Matt exclaimed at supper one night.

Through the door came a low, anxious whine. Then came a long sniff, as White Fang smelled the air to make sure Scott was still inside.

"I do believe that wolf's on to you," said Matt.

"What the devil can I do with a wolf in California?" Scott demanded.

Silence followed. Again came the low, half-sobbing whine and the long, searching sniff.

"There's no denyin' he thinks a lot of you…" began Matt.

"I know what's best," snapped Scott.

Then came the day when, through the open cabin door, White Fang saw the suitcase on the floor. White Fang knew the meaning this time.

That night he lifted the long wolf-howl. He pointed his muzzle to the cold stars and told to them his woe. He knew that Scott was leaving and that he would be left behind.

The next day, two Indians arrived and carried away the luggage. After a while, Scott called White Fang into the cabin.

"I'm hitting the long trail, Wolf," he said gently as he patted him. "Now give me a growl—the last, good, good-bye growl."

But White Fang refused to growl. Instead, and after a sad, searching look, he snuggled in, burrowing his head out of sight between the master's arm and body.

"There she blows!" cried Matt as the steamboat on the Yukon River bellowed. "Get a move on!"

Scott and Matt hurried out the front door, leaving White Fang locked inside.

"You must take good care of him, Matt," Scott said. "Write and let me know how he gets along."

"Sure," the dog-musher answered. "But listen to that, will you!?"

White Fang was howling as dogs howl when their masters lie dead. The men turned and hurried toward the ship.

Onboard, Scott was shaking hands good-bye with Matt, who was preparing to go back ashore. But Matt's hand went limp as he stared at something behind Scott. Scott turned to see. Sitting on the deck of the ship several feet away was White Fang.

White Fang came to Scott when he called him. Fresh-made cuts lined White Fang's muzzle, and a gash oozed between his eyes.

"We plumb forgot the windows," Matt said. "He broke right through 'em!"

Scott was not listening. He was thinking quickly. The ship's whistle hooted. Men were scurrying down the gangplank to the shore. He looked at White Fang, then grasped Matt's hand.

"Good-bye, Matt. About the wolf—you needn't write. *I'll* write to *you* about him…"

Matt understood and smiled.

As Matt went down the gangplank, Scott rubbed between White Fang's ears. "Now growl, Wolf," he said. "Growl."

White Fang did.

From the steamship, White Fang landed in San Francisco and boarded a train, where he was chained in a baggage car with his master's bags and luggage. When he came back out, San Francisco had gone. Before him was the smiling countryside, warm and sunny, lazy and quiet.

There was a carriage waiting, and a man and a woman approached. When the woman's arms wrapped around Scott's neck, White Fang became a raging demon!

Scott kept a tight hold on White Fang. "It's all right, Mother," Scott said. "Wolf thought you were trying to hurt me. He'll learn soon enough."

The bags were taken into the carriage, the man-animals followed, and White Fang ran along behind the carriage.

At the end of fifteen minutes, they reached the grounds of an estate. The carriage swung in through a stone gateway and on between a double row of arched walnut trees.

White Fang had little time to look around. Hardly had the carriage entered the grounds, when an angry collie ran toward him. White Fang was about to attack, until he realized the dog was a female. But the collie sprang.

"Here, Collie!" called the strange man sitting with Scott in the carriage.

Weedon Scott laughed, knowing White Fang would not attack a female dog. "Never mind, Father. The wolf will have to learn many things, and it's just as well that he begins now."

The carriage drove on, and still Collie blocked White Fang's way until he bumped her, knocking her over. The way made clear, he followed on with Collie yelping behind him.

As he rounded the house to the covered porch, White Fang came upon the stopped carriage. Almost immediately, he was knocked from his feet by a large deerhound. White Fang lunged to counterattack this new dog.

It was Collie that saved the hound's life. Just as White Fang was in the act of springing, Collie struck him, and again he was knocked off his feet.

The next moment Scott arrived. With one hand he held White Fang, while the father called off the other two dogs.

"I say, this is a pretty warm hello for a lone wolf from the Arctic," Scott said. "In all his life he's only been known once to go off his feet, and here he's been rolled twice in thirty seconds."

WHITE FANG

"Take Collie inside and leave the wolf and Dick to fight it out," suggested Scott's father. "After that they'll be friends."

"That might result in a funeral," laughed the master, knowing White Fang would show no mercy for another male.

"You mean that...?"

Weedon nodded his head. "I mean just that. I'm afraid Dick would be dead inside one minute—two minutes at the most."

He turned to White Fang. "Come on, you Wolf. It's you that'll have to come inside."

White Fang walked up the steps, keeping his eye on Dick. Once inside the house, he found no other dogs. Then he lay down at his master's feet, contented but on guard.

CHAPTER FIFTEEN

The Scott Estate

Here in Sierra Vista, which was the name of Judge Scott's place, White Fang quickly began to make himself at home. He had no further serious trouble with the dogs. The Scotts had allowed White Fang into the house, so Dick and the other dogs accepted him—and left him alone.

Not so with Collie. Though she accepted him, she continued to pick on him and nip at his legs. White Fang made it a point to keep out of her way. When he saw her, he got up and walked off.

White Fang learned to accept Weedon Scott's family, since they belonged to his master. There was Judge Scott, Weedon's father, and the Judge's

wife, Weedon's mother. There were the master's two sisters, Beth and Mary. There was Weedon Scott's wife, Alice, and his children, Weedon and Maud, toddlers of four and six. White Fang had disliked children ever since they mistreated him in the Indian village. When Scott's children first approached him, he snapped warningly. Scott gave him a sharp word, so White Fang let them pat him—though he didn't like it.

After a time, he grew fond of the family, and would lie on the porch at the Judge's feet as he read the paper. He allowed everyone to pat him. He even began to like the children.

This was a new life in a new land for White Fang. In the Northland, White Fang had hunted for food. He did not know that things were different here in the Santa Clara Valley of the Southland. Sauntering around the corner of the house in the early morning, he came upon a chicken that had escaped from the chicken yard. With a couple of leaps and a flash of teeth, he scooped up the frightened and squawking chicken. It was fat and tender. White Fang licked his chops.

Later in the day, he came upon another stray chicken near the stables. One of the stable hands ran to the rescue with a buggy whip. At the first cut of the whip, White Fang left the chicken to go for the man. The man cried out and staggered backward. He dropped the whip and shielded his throat with his arms. Suddenly, Collie appeared on the scene. Just as she had saved Dick the deerhound's life, she now saved the man's. She rushed upon White Fang as the man escaped into the stables, and White Fang backed away before Collie's wicked teeth.

"He'll learn to leave chickens alone," the master said that evening. "But I can't give him the lesson until I catch him in the act."

Two nights later came the act. After the chickens had gone to roost, White Fang climbed over the fence. A moment later he was inside the henhouse, and the slaughter began.

In the morning, the stableman laid out fifty dead white Leghorn hens for Weedon Scott to see. Angrily, Scott held White Fang's nose down to the hens. At the same time he cuffed him soundly. White Fang never raided a chicken roost again. He had learned the law.

But Judge Scott did not believe that the Wolf was cured. "Once a chicken-killer, always a chicken-killer," he said.

Weedon Scott did not agree with his father. "I'll tell you what I'll do," he challenged. "I'll lock Wolf in with the chickens all afternoon."

"But think of the chickens," said the Judge.

"*And* I'll pay you one dollar gold coin for every chicken he kills," Weedon went on. "But… if, at the end of the afternoon, Wolf has not harmed a chicken, you must solemnly repeat to him, 'Wolf, you are smarter than I thought.' "

The judge agreed to the test.

The whole family watched as White Fang was taken and left with the chickens. The "chicken-killer" simply lay down and went to sleep. Once he got up for a drink of water, but he calmly ignored the chickens. As far as he was concerned, they did not exist. He had learned the law.

He stayed all afternoon, then leaped the fence and sauntered back to the house. And on the porch, before the delighted family, Judge Scott sat face to face with White Fang. Slowly and solemnly, he repeated, "Wolf, you are smarter than I thought."

There was so much to learn. There were cats at the houses the master visited that must be let alone. And there were dogs everywhere that snarled at him and that he must not attack. And then, on the crowded sidewalks, there were persons aplenty. They would stop and look at him and, worst of all, pat him. Cats, dogs, turkeys, people—all these he must let alone. In fact, he began to think that he must leave all live things alone. And then, one day, he saw Dick scare up a jackrabbit and chase it. In the end, White Fang figured out that he must not touch any tame animal. But the other animals—the squirrels, and quail, and rabbits—were creatures of the Wild and were "fair game."

CHAPTER SIXTEEN

The Call of Kind

The months came and went. There was plenty of food and no work in the Southland, and White Fang lived fat and happy. Human kindness was like a sun shining upon him. He flourished like a flower planted in good soil.

And yet he remained somehow different from other dogs. The wolf and the Wild still lingered in him. He never chummed with the Southland dogs. He avoided his own kind and clung to the humans. The dogs feared him and greeted him with snarls, but they left him alone—except for Collie. She continued to annoy him whenever she found it possible.

Otherwise, all things went well for White Fang. Danger and hurt did not lurk everywhere about him. Life was soft and easy.

And he learned to romp and play with the master—to be tumbled down and rolled over. He did not even mind when Weedon would laugh at him. Long before, in his old life, laughter had made him frantic with rage. But he could not be angry with this master. As Weedon played and laughed, White Fang's jaws slightly parted, his lips moved a little, and a look of love and humor came into his eyes. He had learned to laugh.

The master went out on horseback a great deal. One of White Fang's chief duties was to go with him, but with no sleds or harness. He ran alongside, free and happy.

On one of these outings, a rabbit scampered in front of the horse. The horse was startled, and it reared up, throwing Weedon Scott. The master examined his injured leg and found it was broken. White Fang sprang in rage at the horse, thinking it had hurt his master.

"Home! Go home!" the master commanded.

White Fang did not want to desert the master. But again, Weedon commanded him to go home.

White Fang started to go—then returned and whined softly. The master talked to him gently, but seriously. White Fang cocked his ears.

"That's all right, old fellow, you just run along home," said Weedon. "Go on home and tell them what's happened to me," Scott said. "Home with you, you Wolf. Get along home!"

White Fang knew the meaning of "home." He turned and trotted away. Then he stopped and looked back over his shoulder. "Go home!" came the sharp command, and this time he obeyed.

The family was on the porch when White Fang arrived. He came up panting, covered with dust.

"Weedon's back," said Weedon's mother.

The children ran to meet White Fang, but he growled and tried to get past them.

"He makes me nervous around the children," said the children's mother.

"A wolf is a wolf," said Judge Scott. "There's no trusting one."

"But he is not *all* wolf," said young Beth.

"That's what Weedon says," replied the Judge. "But how does he know? Why, he looks—"

He did not finish. White Fang stood before him, growling fiercely.

"Go away! Lie down, sir!" Judge Scott commanded.

White Fang turned to Scott's wife. She screamed with fright as he seized her dress in his teeth and dragged on it till the fabric tore.

"I hope he is not going mad," said Weedon's mother. "I told Weedon that an Arctic animal—"

At this moment, White Fang did something the family had never heard him do before. He began to bark.

"He's trying to speak!" Beth announced.

"Something has happened to Weedon," his wife said earnestly.

They were all on their feet, now. White Fang ran down the steps, looking back for them to follow. He led them to his master, and they helped the injured man home. The "Wolf" had done what no wolf can do. He had barked and made himself understood.

After this event, he found a warmer place in the hearts of the Sierra Vista people. They admitted he was a wise dog—even though he was a wolf. Only Judge Scott refused to accept that White Fang had any dog qualities. To him, the animal was all wolf.

The days came and went. As the days grew shorter and White Fang's second winter in the Southland came on, he made a strange discovery. Collie became playful. He forgot that she had once annoyed him.

One day she led him off on a long chase though the pasture and into the woods. Side by side, White Fang ran with Collie—just as his mother, Kiche, and old One Eye had run long years before in the silent Northland forest.

CHAPTER SEVENTEEN

The Sleeping Wolf

It was about this time that the newspapers were full of the daring escape of a convict from San Quentin prison. He was a ferocious man. He had not been born right, and society had treated him poorly.

In San Quentin he fought the guards and other prisoners. The more fiercely he fought, the more harshly the guards handled him. This only made him fiercer. He was a beast—this Jim Hall.

During Jim Hall's third term in prison, he came up against a guard that was almost as great a beast as he. The guard treated him unfairly, lied about him to the warden, and tormented him.

One day Jim Hall killed this guard. He was sent to a small cell where he stayed for three years—completely alone. He never left. He saw no one. His food was shoved in to him. He growled like a wild animal. He hated all things.

And then, one night, he escaped. Three dead guards marked his trail through the prison to the outer walls. He was hunted day and night with bloodhounds. But Jim Hall had disappeared.

In the meantime, the Scott family nervously read the newspapers. The women were afraid, but Judge Scott laughed—though even he worried. For in his last days as a judge, Jim Hall had stood before him and was sentenced to *fifty years* in prison. And in the courtroom, Jim Hall had sworn that if he ever got free, he would come looking for the judge. Then Jim Hall went off to prison… and escaped.

White Fang knew nothing of all this. But he and Alice, the master's wife, shared a secret. Each night, after all of Sierra Vista had gone to bed, she arose and let in White Fang to sleep in the big hall. Now, the "wolf" was not a "house-dog," so early each morning she slipped down and let him out before the family was awake.

On one such night, while the house slept, White Fang awoke and lay quietly. A strange man had paused at the foot of the staircase. Up that staircase was the family White Fang knew to protect. The strange man's foot lifted.

White Fang gave no warning—and no snarl. Into the air he sprang and landed on the strange man's back, dragging him over backward.

There were revolver shots. A man's voice screamed in horror. Snarling followed, and a smashing and crashing of furniture and glass.

The house awoke in alarm. Weedon and Judge Scott came down the stairs. In the middle of smashed furniture, partly on his side, his face hidden by an arm, lay a man. Weedon turned the man's face upward. He was clearly dead.

"Jim Hall," said Judge Scott.

Then they turned to White Fang. He, too, was lying on his side. His eyes were closed, but the lids lifted to look at them, and the tail tried to wag. Then his eyelids dropped and went shut. His body relaxed and flattened out upon the floor.

"He's done for," muttered the master.

"We'll see about that," said the Judge, as he started for the telephone.

"Frankly, he has one chance in a thousand," announced the surgeon, after he had worked an hour and a half on White Fang. "One broken hind leg, three broken ribs, three bullet wounds, a great loss of blood… I should say he hasn't a chance in ten thousand."

"But he mustn't lose any chance," exclaimed Judge Scott. "Never mind the expense. Put him under X-ray—anything. Weedon, telegraph at once to San Francisco for Doctor Nichols. He must have the advantage of every chance."

White Fang received the best care available. The ladies nursed him. And White Fang won out on that one chance in ten thousand. For he had come from the Wild, where the weak do not survive. He clung to life with an iron will.

He lingered out the weeks in bandages and plaster casts, unable to move about. He slept long hours and dreamed much. Once again he lived in the den with Kiche. Or he crept to the knees of Gray Beaver. He ran from Lip-lip and the puppy pack. He lived again his days with Beauty Smith. At these times he whimpered and snarled in his sleep. The family looked on and said that his dreams were bad.

Then came the day when the last bandage and the last plaster cast were taken off. All Sierra Vista was gathered around. The master rubbed his ears, and the master's wife called him the Blessed Wolf. After several failed attempts, he stood on his four legs, tottering and swaying back and forth.

"The Blessed Wolf!" cheered the women.

"Yes. Blessed Wolf," agreed the Judge. "That will be the name for him."

"He'll have to learn to walk again," said the surgeon, "Take him outside."

Outside he went, like a king, with all the family around. He was very weak. He reached the lawn, rested, and then finally reached the stables. There in the doorway lay Collie with six pudgy puppies playing about her in the sun.

Collie snarled a warning, and White Fang was careful to keep his distance. The master helped one waddling puppy toward him, telling White Fang that all was well.

The puppy sprawled in front of him. White Fang cocked his ears and watched it curiously. Then their noses touched, and he felt the warm little tongue of the puppy on his jowl. White Fang's tongue went out and he licked the puppy's face.

The family clapped their hands and sent up cheers. White Fang was surprised, and looked at them in a puzzled way. The other puppies came sprawling toward him, to Collie's great disgust. He calmly permitted them to clamber and tumble over him as he lay with half-shut, patient eyes, drowsing in the sun.

THE END

JACK LONDON

John (Jack) Griffith London was born in 1876 and grew up in San Francisco. He left school at age fourteen and went on to hold many unusual jobs. He was an "oyster pirate," he worked for the Fish Patrol of San Francisco, and he worked on a seal-hunting ship that took him to Japan. He then traveled around the United States. In 1897, he joined the gold rush in the Klondike, in the far north of Alaska and Canada.

In his early twenties, Jack London knew he wanted to be a writer. He was a self-taught man who read and wrote constantly. He continued to travel, sail, and write—about the slums of London, the South Sea islands, boxing, life in the wilds, and life at sea. Some of his more famous works include *The Call of the Wild* (1903), *The Sea-Wolf* (1904), and *White Fang* (1906), which portray scenes and characters from his own experiences.

Jack London had a rich—sometimes wild—life. It was filled with adventure, but it was also filled with illness and private sadness. He died much too early at the age of forty in 1916.